Horace
and the
Christmas
Mystery

SALLY MAGNUSSON

Illustrated by Norman Stone

BLACK & WHITE PUBLISHING

First published 2014
by Black & White Publishing Ltd
29 Ocean Drive, Edinburgh EH6 6JL

1 3 5 7 9 10 8 6 4 2   14 15 16 17

ISBN 978 1 84502 791 9

ALBA | CHRUTHACHAIL

Designed by Richard Budd Design
Printed and bound in Poland by
www.hussarbooks.pl

A SECRET MESSAGE
FOR READERS

Ask a grown-up 'What is a haggis?' and this is
what they will tell you.

A haggis, they will say, is a dish made from
the mashed insides of a sheep. Scots like eating it
on the birthday of their great poet, Robert Burns,
who wrote a poem about how it gushes out of the
bag like a warm, wet pudding.

Yes, I know. Yuk.

But what would you say if I told you that
the haggis is an animal belonging to a species
as ancient as the unicorn, or the centaur, or the
mighty griffin? Only smaller and fatter and, let's
face it, not so mighty.

What would you say if I told you that greedy
haggis hunters have snatched so many haggises to
boil for dinner that there are only a few left on
the face of the earth?

Perhaps you can imagine what it would feel like to be a lone haggis on the run from those hunters. He would need friends, wouldn't he? He would need animals to protect him, but also human friends to keep his whereabouts secret from the enemy. He would need you.

So, let the grown-ups believe their own story if they want to. I am going to tell you a better one. And once you have read it, please remember to keep our secret safe – or this timid endangered species may be lost forever.

The Author

1

It was Christmas Eve in Acre Valley and Horace the Haggis could hardly contain his excitement. He bounded from one friend's house to the next to see what they were up to.

At Dun Foxin' he found Ferdy, the vegetarian fox, knitting Christmas hats for homeless ducklings. Ferdy's chef Dijon was fluttering around the kitchen.

'Ah, my leetle fat friend,' chirped the robin, 'I 'ave made something just for you. See, hot heather mince pies.'

Chomping six at a time, Horace crunched off happily through the snow. A snowball caught him on the back of the head.

'Ha, ha. Got you,' giggled Martha Mouse from a sledge piled high with Christmas decorations. 'Look at these,' she said proudly.

'I'm off to put them up around Mouse Mountain. Come across later and see.'

Horace chucked a snowball back at her, which missed. He went munching on his way.

Passing the Rookery, he looked up to see Ronald Rook struggling to attach an enormous stocking to the topmost branch of his tree. An extremely long list hung right to the ground.

'Spy-on-Your-Neighbours telescope,' Horace read. 'New pink scarf – very expensive.' And (most alarming of all) 'Opera-Singing Handbook for Beginners.' Horace hoped Santa wouldn't spot that one.

It was time, he decided, to spread some Christmas cheer himself. He took out his bagpipes and a long wail blasted through Acre Valley.

'What's that infernal noise?' boomed a military voice.

Hauling himself out of the snow, Major Mole glared at Horace through earthy spectacles.

Horace looked hurt. 'Major, I'm only gearing up for "The Holly and the Haggis". It's my Christmas special. Or would you prefer "Hark the Herald Haggi Sing"?'

'Good gracious no,' shuddered Major Mole. Then, seeing Horace's face fall, he added, 'A fine carol, my boy, although I

prefer "God Rest Ye, Merry Moleymen" myself. Just need some peace to think. I'm drawing up plans for a reindeer landing site.'

'A what?'

'Place for Santa's sleigh to land. Not everyone has a chimney, you know. Now, why don't you just hop along to Doc Leaf's tree and play him some carols? Do that owl the world of good to wake up early.'

Horace found Doc Leaf already up and practising his Christmas conjuring tricks. The blast of 'Away in the Heather, No Burrow for a Bed' gave the owl such a fright that he dropped his magic wand. A tiny rabbit nipped out from under his top hat and ran away.

'HORACE!' roared Doc Leaf. 'Could you please go and play somewhere else.'

Horace sighed. Then he had an idea. Professor Nut had his own bagpipes. They could play together.

Humming to himself, he headed off merrily to the Secret Loch.

And that is where he made the first dreadful discovery.

2

The door of Nut Tower was hanging off its hinges. Every window was broken. Horace could see bits of chimney on the ground amid dozens of scattered acorns. There was no sign of Professor Nut.

Horace tiptoed inside. An icy wind was pouring in through the smashed windows, making a sheet of paper pinned to the fireplace flutter. There was just one mark on the paper.

Horace felt a tingle of fear. He edged closer.

It was a single letter, painted – as Horace noted with a shiver – the colour of blood. The letter was a **V**.

His heart pounding, Horace tore out of the house. Something awful had happened to Professor Nut. He knew it. Somebody, or something, had dragged the squirrel off and left its menacing mark.

Martha would know what to do. She had lived here much longer than him. She would know the meaning of the sign. Horace raced up the hill towards Mouse Mountain.

And that was the moment his heart almost stopped.

Martha's tiny door was gaping open. A sprig of holly lay trampled on the ground and the wind had carried forlorn scraps of tinsel into the nearby bushes.

'Martha!' shouted Horace. 'MARTHA! Where are you?'

There was no reply.

Horace looked around desperately. Then he saw it. Fluttering like a flag from a stick planted in the snow was a sheet of paper. It bore a single letter. **V**.

3

Up the hill at Nettle Farm Angus McPhee was in trouble.

'Call that puny twig a Christmas tree!' his wife was screeching. 'Out you go and get me a decent one or there's no turkey for you. And take that mangy cat with you.'

Mrs McPhee was the only one who could strike fear into Horace's arch-enemy, the chief of the haggis-hunters.

'Certainly, my dear,' wheedled Angus McPhee nervously. 'I know just where to find a better tree. The finest in the forest. Just let me find my axe and I'll be off.'

'You'd better, you useless oaf. And while you're at it, get me a haggis for our Christmas starter. You've been promising me a juicy one for months.'

'Yes, babykins. Right away, my dove,' soothed McPhee. 'Come on, Cat. Let's go.'

The farmer and his Cat with No Name trudged outside.

4

Horace arrived breathlessly at Ferdy's house. He burst in through the door.

'Ferdy! Dijon! Something terrible's happened. Martha's gone and Professor Nut, too. Someone's left a warning sign – it's a . . .'

He trailed off. There was no one there. A pile of tiny pom-pom hats had unravelled across the doorway. A tray-load of gingerbread foxes lay broken on the floor.

Horace looked around with dread. He knew what he was going to find. Except that this time there were two squares of paper – two horrible Vs pinned side by side to the wall.

Horace stumbled out and along the burn, his fur prickling with fear. One by one his friends were vanishing. He had no idea where they were or what had befallen them. He sat down and put his head in his hands.

He was too dazed to notice a huge sign:
'SLEIGH LANDING ZONE. KEEP OUT!'

'Horace, my dear haggis, what's wrong?'
barked a familiar voice.

'Oh, Major Mole, thank goodness you're
safe,' said Horace, throwing his arms around the
mole and knocking his glasses off.

'Safe? Of course I'm safe. What are you
talking about? I've been out here constructing
this fine airfield. What do you think of the
carrots?'

A long area had been cleared of snow to
make a runway. Four large carrots were hanging
from a group of trees at the end.

'That'll pull the reindeer in,' the mole said
proudly.

Horace wasn't interested.

'Major, it's Martha, and Ferdy, and Dijon,
and Professor Nut. They're gone. Vanished. And
there was a sign left behind. A **V.** A single **V.**
Looked as if it had been written in blood.'

Major Mole went as pale as his fur would
allow. 'Not a **V**?' he gasped.

'You mean you kn-kn-know what it means?' stuttered Horace.

Major Mole opened his mouth and shut it again. 'No, it can't be,' he said at last. 'They left.'

'Who did? Who left where? You've got to tell me.'

'I'll tell you,' rasped another voice. Ronald Rook had flapped on to a branch behind them. He was looking at Horace with the smirk he always saved for bad news. 'V, my friend, is for "Vole". And not just any vole. It's the secret sign of Don Volio, godfather of the most dangerous mob of gangsters Acre Valley has ever known.'

Horace sat down hurriedly.

Ronald lowered his voice. 'The Major's right. The gang pulled out a while back. Things were getting too hot for them. But they're back. Their lair is deep inside the Darkling Forest – a place no decent animal would ever venture into.'

The rook's eyes gleamed. 'Be afraid, Horace,' he squawked with gloomy relish. 'The Boss is back and V is his sign.'

5

Major Mole's colour had returned. He puffed up his chest.

'Right, men, this calls for action,' he said, addressing a tree stump. He hadn't found his glasses yet. Horace nudged him.

'Ah yes, there you are.' He swung around and directed his words at a bush instead. 'As a war-hero (did I ever mention my fearless exploits in the Battle of the Ghost Dog?) I am not going to let any jumped-up vole make our friends vanish. I propose we gather the troops, enter enemy territory and carry out an ambush.'

Ronald looked appalled. 'Er, no need to be hasty, Major. Horace isn't the bravest of haggises and I have my singing career to consider. Perhaps we could think about it after Christmas . . .'

Major Mole opened his mouth to argue. But

before he could, Horace stepped forward shakily.

'Martha and Ferdy have always stood up for me,' he said in a quavery voice. 'Now it's my turn. Lead on, Major.'

'Lead on? LEAD ON?' screeched Ronald. 'Have you any idea what the Darkling Forest is like?' He shuddered. 'It's dark. Cold. Wild. Mysterious.' His voice rose hysterically. 'A place where terrible secrets lurk behind every tree.'

'Drama queen,' muttered Major Mole under his breath.

Horace didn't like the sound of this forest at all. But he took a big breath. 'I've spent my whole life running away,' he said, wishing he could do exactly that right now. 'It's time to be brave.'

'Bravo, my boy,' said Major Mole, facing the right way at last and clapping Horace on the back. 'Now let's get ourselves armed to meet these ruffians.'

'Armed?' Ronald gulped. 'You mean weapons?'

'Of course I do, you annoying bird,' said the Major. 'Here, take this.' He handed Ronald a plastic fly swatter. 'And I shall lead from the front with my trusty twig.'

'And I've got the very thing, too,' shouted Horace. He pulled out the hair gel he always carried in his pouch and tried a practice squirt, narrowly missing Major Mole's left eye.

The Mole Patrol lined up for action, a couple of old forks at the ready. Nobby the Newt reluctantly attached a small pebble to his tail, hoping no vole would notice.

The small band straggled forward. Stacey and Tracey Magpie hopped from branch to branch beside them, excitedly tweeting every movement on their phones.

Ronald hovered overhead, swishing the fly swatter with such energy that he knocked Major Mole's helmet off.

'Fool of a rook!' snapped the Major.

On their way to the Darkling Forest they passed Doc Leaf's oak tree.

'Oh no,' said Horace, fear clutching his heart again. 'Not another one.'

The owl was gone. His magic wand lay abandoned in the snow. On his door was pinned a **V**.

6

Angus McPhee was sharpening his axe on a grinding-stone in the barn. Sparks flew. The Cat with No Name was inspecting her claws lovingly.

'Right, Cat,' the farmer grumbled, 'if there's to be any Christmas dinner for us tomorrow, we'd better get moving.'

He hoisted the axe over his shoulder and the pair set off across the fields in the direction of the Darkling Forest. Dusk was falling on Christmas Eve.

Ahead lay the thick plantation of trees marking the limit of Acre Valley. It looked dark and dangerous. Even the Cat shivered.

There was one tree in the distance that stood taller than the rest. It seemed to Angus McPhee that there was a curious glow about it.

'That's the tree for us, Cat,' he said. 'It's as good as calling to us. Mrs McPhee won't be able to say a word against that one.'

The axe glinted as the pair made their way into the shadows.

'And keep your eyes peeled for the haggis,' added Farmer McPhee. 'Catch that one and we'll have our best Christmas ever.'

The Cat smirked nastily.

7

'Silence, men,' whispered Major Mole, stopping so suddenly that everybody bumped into the one in front.

Nobby's pebble flew from the end of his tail and knocked off the Major's helmet again. Horace squeezed his tube in fright and sent a jet of hair gel into Tracey Magpie's eye. Stacey found it so funny that she just had to tweet the news.

'I hope you're not giving away our position to the enemy, Stacey,' snapped the Major. 'Those voles have master codebreakers in their ranks, you know.'

Stacey rolled her eyes and kept tapping.

They moved forward again. The Darkling Forest was closing in on them now, blanking out the last of the day's light. The wind rustled eerily through trees that felt too close together.

The snow on the branches gave everything a ghostly air.

Nobby had given up pretending to be brave and ducked into Horace's empty pouch. Horace could feel the newt's little heart thumping.

Suddenly there was the crack of a branch and a quick rustling in the undergrowth. Strange shadows flitted among the trees.

'Shh!' ordered the Major. 'We're being stalked. Weapons at the ready!'

But it was too late. Suddenly everything went dark. Utterly and completely black.

Horace could hear Major Mole shouting, 'Get that sack off my head, you blathering brigand. Don't you know I'm an officer in Her Majesty's Underground Services?'

Horace put a hand up to his own head and found it covered with rough sacking. He couldn't see a thing.

A harsh voice behind him barked, 'Get moving or I'll make ya. D'ya understand?'

Horace stumbled blindly forward. He felt trees closing in on either side. They were being led deeper and deeper into the forest.

'You wouldn't hurt me in cold blood, would you?' he stammered.

'Nah,' answered the voice with a menacing laugh, 'I'd let ya warm up a little first.'

Inside Horace's pouch Nobby the newt fainted.

8

At last they were all ordered to halt. Rough
hands removed the sacks from their heads.

'Hey, guys, look what we found creeping
up on us with their weapons,' rasped their captor.
'Just as well Evolina was checking
that Twitter thing of hers or
they might have caught us
nappin'.'

With the sack off,
Horace could
see who was
speaking –
an enormous,
muscly vole
with a mean
expression.
Horace gulped.

He hadn't known there were voles that big.
Dozens of others crowded around.

'Someone go and get da Boss,' ordered the
giant vole. 'Da Boss is gonna be angry and ya
won't like it, I tell ya, when da Boss gets angry.'

'Angry?' squawked Ronald.

'Ya better believe it, pointy beak. We voles
don't like folk sneakin' up on us, specially when
we's trying to be nice.'

'Nice?' exploded the Major. 'You call
kidnapping innocent animals *nice*?'

He didn't have a chance to say any more.
Suddenly all the voles fell silent. A loud, breathy
whisper filled the clearing.

'WHO DARES . . . TO COME . . . INTO
MY HOME . . . BRINGING WEAPONS . . .
AGAINST MY FAMILY?'

Horace began to tremble. Nobby
whimpered. Even Major Mole's twig drooped.
They all held their breaths.

The voles parted. The deadly gangster boss
was coming. Stomp. Stomp. Stomp. A cheer went
up from the voles.

Horace looked around.

Where *was* this monster? He couldn't see anyone at all.

'Hey, you!'

Horace looked down. At his feet stood an extremely fat vole in a soft-brimmed hat. His eyes were hidden behind dark shades. He was *tiny*.

'What d'ya mean by bringing war to Vole Hollow when I, Don Volio, invited you here in peace?' demanded the roly-poly figure in a chilling voice. 'Speak, haggis. Whatcha up to?'

Peace? Horace was more and more

confused. 'We . . . we were looking for our friends,' he stuttered.

'Your friends? You wanna see your friends, do you?' Don Volio snapped his fingers. 'Vinny, show 'em!'

The big muscly vole heaved on a rope and the branches in front of them were pulled apart. Horace could hardly believe what he saw.

Light blazed from the clearing. An enormous fir tree, laden with fairy lights, stretched up towards the dark sky. And there, in the cockpit of a crane at the top of the tree, was Professor Nut. The crane's mechanical arm was fixing a silver star in place with the help of a huge metal hand.

'Hello, Horace,' Professor Nut shouted down. 'Do you like my acorn-picker? I wondered when you'd get here.'

Dijon the robin was fluttering around importantly. 'Ah, 'Orace, at last I have the chance to show these voles some French cooking. All they seem to cook here is pasta.'

Doc Leaf was perched on one of the lower

branches, showing Ferdy Fox a card trick. Ferdy waved cheerily.

Martha was darting around with a heap of decorations in her arms, chattering to a little vole in pigtails and a judo costume.

'Horace!' she squeaked. 'Come and meet my new friend Evolina Vole. She's a judo black belt.'

Horace and Major Mole looked at each other, dumbstruck. What on earth was going on?

Then Horace spotted a long table in front of the tree. It was loaded with every kind of food, including, he noticed at once, a huge bowl of pink heather.

At every place lay a Christmas cracker. And propped in front of each cracker stood a card with a guest's name above a single letter. The letter **V**.

Don Volio waved his fist at Horace.

'I . . . AM . . . ANGRY,' he whispered hoarsely.

Ronald Rook shot up the Christmas tree and disappeared.

'I am very, very angry.'

9

Don Volio's eyes glittered behind his dark glasses as he glared at Horace.

'I came to Acre Valley in peace – in peace, I tell ya – to make amends for times past. And you come here wid weapons of war. Sticks. Stones. Hair gel.'

He snapped his fingers. 'Ya've messed with us, trumpet nose. So now maybe we gonna mess with you. Vinny!'

The giant vole crunched his knuckles. 'Ready, Boss.'

Horace shuddered.

'Please don't be hasty, Mr Volio, sir,' he said in a trembling voice. 'My friends were kidnapped. I admit they don't seem to mind very much, but you left your secret sign, dripping in blood, and I thought . . .'

'Kidnapped!' roared Don Volio. 'Secret sign!

Blood! Is that how ya describe my Christmas poity invitation in my nice red Christmassy ink?'

'Party invitation?' repeated Horace.

'I sent one to you, too,' said the Boss bitterly. 'And to that stoopid mole. Didn't ya find it in your house, like the others, with the address on the back?'

'I wasn't in my burrow,' said Horace, beginning to get the picture. 'And I never looked on the other side of the paper.'

Suddenly he thought of something. 'But why was Professor Nut's house all smashed up?'

'Because we needed that silly nut's Acorn Crane, of course, to get the decorations up the tree. And the crazy squirrel, he hit the wrong button and drove it backwards into his own house.'

'Why was Ferdy's house in such a mess, then? And Martha's place?'

'Oh, those guys were just in a hurry to get here. The kooky French redbreast couldn't wait to poke his beak into my spaghetti pan. And that new friend of Evolina's, she raced over here on

31

her sledge to help with the decorations just as soon as she saw the invitation.'

There was an excited squeak from the tree. 'Isn't it lovely, Horace?'

Horace looked over to where Martha and Evolina were adding their final touches. Evolina was leaping Tarzan-like from branch to branch with the tinsel.

Horace bent down and held out his hand to Don Volio. 'Well, sir, I can only say sorry for making a mistake.'

Don Volio still looked suspicious, but he shook hands gruffly.

Horace patted his stomach. 'And is that, by any chance, a bowl of heather you've kindly prepared?' Congratulating himself on a tricky situation well handled, he made for the table.

But at that moment another of Don Volio's henchmen rushed into the glade.

'Boss, Boss, we got trouble,' he panted. 'Big, BIG trouble.'

10

The Cat was getting fed up. They had been
trailing through the Darkling Forest for ages. She
was tired and hungry. A nice fat mouse for supper
would go down nicely. Even a vole would do.

'Almost there, Cat,' said Farmer McPhee.
'Just through these bushes. My, that tree's
bright.'

He gave his axe a practice swing. 'I'll have
it chopped down in no time.'

The axe gleamed, and so did the farmer's
eyes. 'And if anything gets in my way,' he
muttered, 'I'll chop that too.'

The Cat skipped further away.

Funny, she was thinking, how brightly lit
the forest seemed to be now. And what was that
she could smell? Wasn't that . . . MOUSE?

The Cat sprang forward, teeth bared. The
farmer crashed through the bushes behind her.

Then they stopped in amazement.

There in the clearing was the tall fir tree. It was ablaze with light and Christmas colour, with a silver star twinkling at the top.

But that's not what made Angus McPhee smile his most horrible smile or the Cat lick her lips and narrow her cold eyes.

No, what she saw were voles, enough to keep her in dinners for weeks. And in their midst – even better – was that upstart Martha Mouse, who had got the better of her in the Battle of Nettle Farm. Oh, revenge was going to be very, very sweet.

Angus McPhee paid no attention to the voles scattering before his great, clumping boots. What he saw was something else. This animal's hand was clutching a large sprig of heather.

34

This animal was staring at him as if a terrible nightmare had just come true. This animal was going to be his at last.

With a great bellow of triumph McPhee pounded across the glade towards Horace the Haggis.

11

You don't get to be Boss of the most feared family in Acre Valley without knowing how to keep your cool. Don Volio stood his ground and issued an order.

'Vinny, get moving wid that tinsel. Meatball, grab the other end.'

The two voles sprang forward.

'Have a pleasant trip,' sneered Don Volio, as McPhee went flying over the tinsel and across the table. His head ended up in a vat of spaghetti.

Now the farmer was really furious. He hauled himself off the table, tightened his grip on the axe and whirled towards Horace again.

'I'll get you this time, haggis,' he yelled. 'You'll be on my dinner plate tomorrow or my name's not Angus McPhee.'

'And *you'll* be on *my* dinner plate,' hissed the Cat, stalking towards Martha, who stood frozen with fear beneath the Christmas tree.

'I seem to remember you once called me a Stinky Toilet Brush,' said the Cat silkily. 'I don't like mice who talk to me like that.'

'No?' said a cool voice behind her. 'Perhaps you'd prefer Weedy Whiskers? Or Old Smelly Breath? Or how about, let's see, Balloon-Sized Bottom? All of which, by the way, you have.'

'WHAT?' The Cat swung round, fuming
with rage. What she saw was Evolina Vole
casually tightening her black judo belt.

The Cat raised her paw to strike. But that
was as far as she got. Evolina caught
it in her own tiny paw, twirled the

Horace and the Christmas Mystery

Cat around, grabbed her tail and flung her to
the ground in a perfect judo throw. Martha
gaped – and then danced with joy.

The Cat saw stars – and they weren't
the kind on the Christmas tree.

Smiling grimly, Evolina rolled up
her sleeves and strode towards
her again.

The farmer was still chasing Horace. Round and round the table they raced.

Nobby the newt tried to help by firing squirts of hair gel from Horace's pouch.

Ferdy Fox snapped at McPhee's heels. Tracey and Stacey Magpie pecked at his hair.

But nothing was working. Angus McPhee was determined to catch his prey this time.

'Help!' shouted Horace, racing round the table, his heart thumping with terror. 'He's going to get me!'

Major Mole was not getting very far fighting with his twig, which one or two of the voles had laughed at rather unkindly. Just then an acorn landed on his helmet and he peered upwards.

'Aha!' he muttered, unable to see a thing as usual. 'An army tank, I'll be bound. What's it doing up there? Never mind, just what we need.' He waved across at the magpies.

'Air support!' he bellowed. 'Get me up there.'

Tracey and Stacey swooped to his side at

once. Clutching a shoulder each, they hauled the Major to the top of the tree and dropped him safely into the cabin of the crane beside an astonished Professor Nut.

'Mole's in control,' barked the Major. 'My, this takes me back. Now, move aside, Nut, while I find out how this tank attacks. Here we go. Three-two-one FIRE!'

He flicked the biggest lever he could find. A loud creak sounded around Vole Hollow as the huge mechanical arm began to move.

12

Down below, Horace was tiring. Angus McPhee sensed his moment had come at last. It would be haggis and turkey for Christmas dinner for sure.

'Got you!' he yelled.

But McPhee should have looked up. As he made a last lunge for Horace, he felt a tug at his back. Two huge metal fingers were attaching themselves to his braces.

'What ho!' cried Major Mole, waving from the cabin of the Acorn Crane. 'Now, I wonder what this switch does.'

Slowly the mechanical arm creaked up again. This time, dangling from its fingers hung a wriggling, red-faced farmer.

'Help!' yelled Angus McPhee, as he was lifted into the sky. 'I'm scared of heights.'

Up and up he was yanked. Desperately he flung out a hand to grab a branch of the tree.

'Ouch!' Pine needles jabbed him, but he held on.

The mechanical arm pulled even harder.

The farmer's elastic braces were stretched further and further.

'Help me, Cat, you useless bag of fleas,' he yelled. 'I can't hold on much longer.'

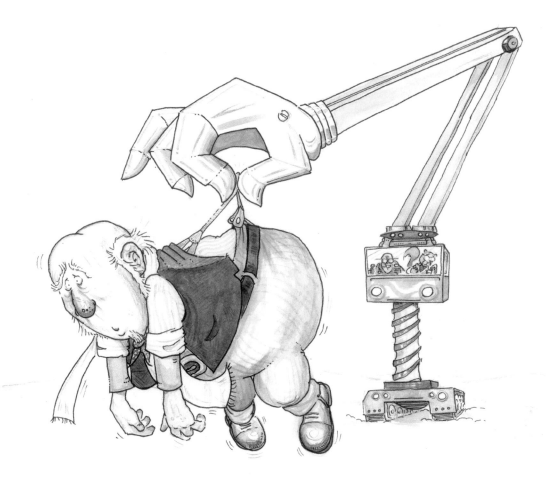

But the Cat couldn't help. She was being whirled round and round so fast by Evolina Vole that she felt she was about to take off.

The next moment Evolina let go and the Cat *did* take off.

At that very second Angus McPhee let go of the branch. With a mighty twang of braces he was catapulted across the clearing and over the trees.

The Cat zoomed into the sky beside him and the pair soared across the valley together.

Evolina rubbed her hands and adjusted her judo tunic. Martha waved them off cheekily.

'Bye bye, you two,' she giggled. 'So sorry you had to fly.'

13

Everyone watched in amazement as Angus
McPhee and the Cat with No Name flew out
of the clearing. Horace was feeling extremely
shaky. Phew! That was close.

Don Volio strode forward and clapped his
hands. 'Now da business is outta da way, it's time
to have da poity. Bring on da feast.'

A team of voles rushed forward, carrying
more piles of food. The table groaned with jellies
and cakes and great mounds of ice cream.

Horace tried a scoop of heather ice cream
and thought he had gone to heaven. Doc Leaf
allowed the rabbit to hop out of his hat and taste
some leaf-flavoured jelly. Evolina tackled the
giant Vinny in an arm wrestle – and won, of
course.

Major Mole was still picking himself out of
the snow, having discovered the crane's ejector

seat by accident and landed with a bump.

'Humph,' he grumbled. 'They don't make tanks like they used to.'

Only Martha had not moved at all. She kept looking at the sky.

'Don't worry,' Horace said gently, 'they've gone now.'

'It's not them I'm looking at,'
Martha squeaked. 'There's
something else up there.
Look, everyone!'

They all gazed upwards. Away to the north
of the forest a light had appeared. A faint jingly
sound drifted towards them in the night air.
A few moments later a huge sleigh, laden with
parcels, passed overhead. A large round figure in
red at the reins waved to them.

'By Jove,' said Major Mole. 'It's Santa,

heading for my landing site. I knew those carrots would do the trick.'

Horace took out his bagpipes. Before anyone could stop him, the strains of 'We Wish You a Merry Christmas' blasted around Vole Hollow and out across Acre Valley.

And for once his friends loved it. Across the valley everyone burst into Christmas song.

Well, not quite everyone.

In a damp field two cold, miserable creatures were hauling themselves out of a soggy old haystack.

There was a light in the window of Nettle Farm, but not a very welcoming one. Mrs McPhee was waiting.

The End

MAP
of
ACRE VALLEY

DARKLING FOREST

DEE

MOLE
HILL

ROOKERY

HORACE'S
BURROW

DUCK
POND

DUN
FOXIN'

DAFFODIL
MEADOW